Colors

Written by Felicia Law
Illustrated by Paula Knight

NORWOOD HOUSE PRESS

Chicago, Illinois

DEAR CAREGIVER

The **Patchwork** series is a whimsical collection of books that integrate poetry to reinforce primary concepts among emergent readers. You might consider these modern-day nursery rhymes that are relevant for today's children. For example, rather than a Miss Muffet sitting on a tuffet, eating her curds and whey, your child will encounter a Grandma and Grandpa dancing a Samba, or a big sister who knows how to make rocks skim and the best places to swim.

Not only do the poetry and prose within the **Patchwork** books help children broaden their understanding of the concepts and recognize key words, the rhyming text helps them develop phonological awareness—an underlying skill necessary for success in transitioning from emergent to conventional readers.

 As you read the text, invite your child to help identify the words that rhyme, start and end with similar sounds, or find the words connected to the pictures. The pictures in these books feature illustrations resembling the technique of torn-paper collage. The artwork can inspire young artists to experiment with torn-paper to create images and write their own poetry.

Above all, the most important part of the reading experience is to have fun and enjoy it!

Sincerely,

Shannon Cannon

Shannon Cannon, Ph.D.
Literacy Consultant

Norwood House Press • P.O. Box 316598 • Chicago, Illinois 60631
For more information about Norwood House Press please visit our website at
www.norwoodhousepress.com or call 866-565-2900.

LIBRARY OF CONGRESS CATALOGING-IN-PUBLICATION DATA
Law, Felicia.
  Colors / by Felicia Law ; illustrated by Paula Knight.
    pages cm. -- (Patchwork)
  Summary: Torn paper collages and simple, rhyming text portray children enjoying colors in many different forms, from the yellow of a sunflower to the black of the night sky. Includes a word list.
  ISBN 978-1-59953-709-2 (library edition : alk. paper) -- ISBN 978-1-60357-807-3 (ebook)
[1. Stories in rhyme. 2. Colors--Fiction.] I. Knight, Paula, illustrator. II. Title.
  PZ8.3.L3544Col 2015
  [E]--dc23
                                    2014047191

274N—062015
Manufactured in the United States of America in North Mankato, Minnesota.

Oops!

whoops!

brown gloops

3

Sunflowers

The flowers lift their faces
They open one by one
The children lift their faces
To catch the golden sun

The flowers stretch golden petals
To catch the warmth and light
The children stretch on tiptoe
To match the sunflowers' height

Green crocodile

Make way!

Step aside!

Don't delay!

Run and hide!

Here comes a

Jaw snapping

Claw trapping

Mean green crocodile!

7

Little worm

I told

The little worm

That my favorite color

Was pink

The worm agreed with me

I think!

Blue waves

Sitting here

At the edge of the blue blue sea

There's just the blue blue sky

The blue blue birds

The blue blue waves

And me

11

Ketchup

Just one little squeeze

And red ketchup

Can end up

All over the place

All over the cat

All over the mat

All over the hat

Splat!

12

Purple paint

Red paints
Paint red

Blue paints
Paint blue

Mix them into purple
Purple paints
YOU!

Snowy day

Each time I scrunched
   the crisp white snow
Into a ball
   And let it go
Hitting the snowman 'Smack'
   on the nose
Where it melted in drips
   And slowly froze

The snowman
   Hit me back
      'Thwack!'

17

The ball room

Plastic and yellow

Spongy like jello

I love bouncing

In the ball room

Slipping and flipping

Jumping and bumping

Flopping and toppling

Stumbling and tumbling

Sliding and hiding

Wriggling and giggling

I love bouncing

In the ball room

18

19

Black

Stars that twinkle

Lights that show

Eyes that sparkle

Bugs that glow

Tiny pinpoints

Fade and grow

Even on the darkest night

A sky of black is full of light

This book includes these concept words:

- ball
- bird
- black
- blue
- brown
- children
- crocodile
- eye
- face
- flower
- golden
- green

○ light	● red	● sunflower
● little	○ sea	● wave
● paint	● sky	● white
● petal	● snow	○ worm
○ pink	● star	● yellow
● purple	○ sun	

23